Alien Deeps

by

Douglas Hill

Illustrated by Harriet Buckley

For Kelsey and Cale

First published 2000 in Great Britain by
Barrington Stoke Ltd
10 Belford Terrace, Edinburgh EH4 3DQ
Copyright © 2000 Douglas Hill
Illustrations © Harriet Buckley

Reprinted 2001, 2003

ISBN 1-902260-55-4
Printed by Polestar AUP Aberdeen Ltd

A Note from the Author

Why do I write science fiction and fantasy? Because I loved to read them when I was young, when I discovered how they can blast your imagination wide open in wildly exciting ways. At the same time, I started dreaming of being an author.

Years later, I came to live in Britain (from Canada) to try to make my dream of being an author come true. Before long, I got the chance to try out my favourite sort of writing - science fiction and fantasy. And I'm still happily at it, dreaming up strange futures, worlds of magic and faraway planets.

In *Alien Deeps* it's a watery planet, with secrets. Take a deep breath ...

Contents

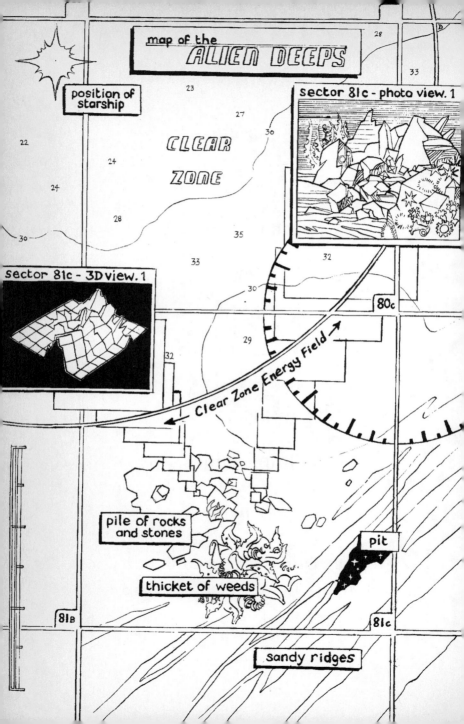

Chapter 1
Bending the Rules

Tal slowed down and let himself drift through the murky water towards the ocean floor. An alarm light had started blinking inside the helmet of his subsuit.

"All *right*," he grumbled aloud as he scowled at the light. "I *know* where I am."

The light was reminding him that he was coming to the edge of the Clear Zone. The Zone was surrounded by an energy field, for protection.

Because the ocean lay on an alien planet, far from Earth.

The Clear Zone was a huge area around the starship that had brought human explorers – including Tal – to that planet. The energy field kept ocean creatures out of the Zone.

So far the humans hadn't found any dangerous creatures in the ocean. But they had been there for only a month and they were taking no chances.

The energy field wasn't designed to *hurt* the creatures. It only shocked them a little, to turn them away. If Tal swam through it, he wouldn't feel a thing inside his subsuit.

But if he left the Clear Zone, the energy field would cut off his suit's netcom link with the starship. If anything went wrong, he wouldn't be able to call for help. That was why no one from the ship, scientists or crew, was allowed to swim alone outside the Clear Zone.

And Tal, who was just thirteen, shouldn't even have been anywhere near the *edge* of the Zone. In fact he wasn't allowed to swim out of sight of the starship.

But he had got bored with always swimming in the same area, looking at the

same underwater things. He had started to explore farther away, a little farther each time. Everyone on the ship was busy with their work, so no one noticed.

That day, Tal had swum all the way to the protected edge of the Zone and he was enjoying the excitement of being where he wasn't supposed to be.

Still drifting, he touched a switch on his helmet to shut off the flashing alarm that was warning him he was on the edge of the Clear Zone. As he peered through his face-plate he saw a faint shimmer ahead. It was the energy field at the edge of the Zone.

Then he touched a larger switch, to turn on his helmet light. In its brightness he saw something much more interesting.

On the other side of the energy field, not far away, he saw a large pile of rocks jumbled together with smaller stones. Many of the rocks were covered with thick, tufty moss, coloured bright red and yellow.

In a shadowy space among the rocks, Tal glimpsed a movement. "That's no plant," he muttered to himself. "That's something *swimming*."

The moving thing vanished among the rocks, as if afraid of his light. But Tal kept staring. He felt curious and excited, as he swam forward. It hadn't looked very big, he thought. And if it was afraid of his light, it probably wasn't dangerous.

Also, the heap of rocks wasn't *too* far from the edge of the Clear Zone and the safety of the energy field ...

So, he thought, why not bend the rules a little more? Why not go *across* just for a minute and have a look?

His heart was beating faster as he plunged forward through the protecting energy field on the edge of the Zone.

Out into the unknown waters of the alien sea.

Chapter 2
Surrounded

Tal didn't have to work hard at swimming, because his subsuit was powered. It was a bit like a spacesuit, with a steely-tough outer skin. When the power was switched off, the subsuit was stiff and heavy, almost like a suit of armour. When the power was on, it became as light and flexible as cloth.

The power source was in a small backpack. It had micro-jets that could push him through the water as slowly as a turtle, or as swiftly as a dolphin. Also, the backpack held filters that took oxygen from the water like a fish's gills and a little tank that stored air in case of emergencies.

So Tal wasn't thinking about his safety, even in the forbidden waters beyond the Clear Zone.

He was far more interested in the mysterious moving thing, hiding in the heap of rocks ahead.

"I hope you're still there, whatever you are," he muttered.

The scientists from the starship had

been exploring day and night. They had also sent out robot drones to explore. And they had found plenty of strange things swimming or scuttling through the dim waters. But all of those creatures were small and harmless.

Still, the scientists knew, it was a huge ocean. The planet was almost *all* ocean. And the human explorers had so far looked at only a tiny bit of it.

"For all we know," Tal's Dad kept saying, "the place could be full of monsters!"

Tal's Dad was an expert on alien life, which was why he was on the expedition. And, as there was no one else to look after Tal, he had gone along too.

On the starship, he helped where he could with simple jobs for his Dad and the other scientists.

But he was usually left on his own after his jobs were done, when everyone else was still at work. Of course he had schoolwork to do, using his Compu-Tutor. But more often, he went swimming.

And this was the best swim of all. Tal felt like a true space adventurer, exploring out beyond the protected Zone – searching for an alien life form.

"What if it's something new, that no one has seen yet?" he whispered smiling to himself. "Wouldn't Dad be jealous ..."

When Tal reached the heap of rocks, it looked even bigger from close up. But he could see nothing moving.

"Come on," he muttered to the unseen creature. "Show yourself."

But then his helmet light showed him an opening among the rocks. It was a small cave, where the colourful moss grew thickly, glowing in his light.

Tal wanted a handful of moss, as a souvenir. So he swam on into the cave. Suddenly he gave a gasp that was almost a shriek.

He was surrounded – by a forest of snaky, wriggling, alien tentacles.

Chapter 3
Unwelcome Company

Just as quickly, his fright drained away.

"Octo-clowns!" he gasped, weak with relief.

Octo-clowns were small creatures with round heads the size of melons and tiny, puffy bodies. Tal's Dad had given them their name – because each of them had eight

15

long, thin tentacles, like an octopus. And each one had a big, round, bright red nose.

Also, every octo-clown had strange patches of skin around its large eyes. The patches glowed with bright colours and flashed on and off like neon signs.

Tal gave a shaky laugh. "Sorry, clowns," he said, although he knew they couldn't hear him through his helmet. "My light must have scared you. But that makes us even – because you scared me, too."

He guessed the octo-clowns were feeding on the coloured moss. But as he backed out of the cave, the creatures followed him. And they kept patting and prodding him with the delicate tips of their tentacles.

16

Octo-clowns always did that. Tal's Dad thought it was a way they had of sensing things, as if the tentacles were like the feelers of insects. Still, it got a bit annoying after a while.

"Leave off, now," he muttered, pushing gently with his gloved hands at the puffy little bodies. "Go on back to your moss."

But still the octo-clowns swarmed around him. And then Tal realised that the creatures weren't simply touching him. They seemed to be trying to take *hold* of him, twining their tentacles around his arms and legs, feebly *pulling* at him.

Still, they seemed too funny and delicate and harmless to be any kind of threat. And he was sure that his subsuit's power could

17

easily break free of their grasp, if he wanted.

So Tal went with them, the way they seemed to want him to go. That way led around some boulders, to the far side of the heap of rocks. There Tal saw another group of octo-clowns with their eye patches flashing wildly.

When he got closer, he saw why they seemed disturbed. A smaller octo-clown, probably a young one, was in trouble. One of its tentacles was trapped under a big rock, which somehow must have toppled over on top of it.

The others, even all working together, weren't strong enough to move the rock. So they were asking Tal to help them.

"Out of the way, then," he said, brushing octo-clowns aside as he moved forward.

It wasn't that big a rock and everything weighs less underwater. Tal gripped it and heaved. With the suit's power helping him, the rock rolled away quite easily.

At once the other octo-clowns gathered up the little rescued one. Then they whisked away at amazing speed until they vanished into the water's dimness.

"You could have said thank you!" Tal muttered, half-smiling.

Then he gazed around. That area, beyond the rocks, had lots of interesting dips and cracks in the ocean floor, with strange plants growing everywhere.

Tal knew that he should get straight back into the Clear Zone. But he decided to explore for a few moments longer, starting with a patch of tall, feathery weeds that sprouted nearby.

Among the weeds he found some flowering vines that grew in perfect coils. And he chased a tiny skittering creature with a blue shell and many legs, which buried itself instantly when he got too near.

Then, as he came out of the weeds on the far side, he froze with sudden shock once again.

A short distance ahead, he saw three humans in subsuits, who somehow seemed to be rising up out of the ocean floor.

Chapter 4
Mysterious Pit

Tal drew back among the weeds and stared. The three had to be from the starship, but he couldn't tell who they were. Subsuits all looked alike and Tal was too far away to see their faces through their face-plates.

He also couldn't work out where they had just appeared from. And one of them was carrying a large, plastic sack – another mystery.

But Tal's main concern was to keep out of sight. The three figures were swimming towards the weeds where he was hiding. And he was outside the Clear Zone, against orders. He would be in deep trouble if anyone from the ship found him there.

Tal tried not to move or blink. But he twitched inside his subsuit when, without warning, he heard a loud, harsh voice.

"Comin' up like that always makes me sweat," the voice snarled. "Never knowin' who might be around."

Tal caught his breath. One of the mystery trio was speaking over a helmet netcom. The netcoms in subsuits were made to be switched on all the time, for safety reasons. So Tal, through *his* netcom, could hear what the others said.

Of course they wouldn't expect anyone to be listening. They were outside the energy field that cut off netcom contact with the starship. But Tal had to try to be invisible and to breathe silently. If he could hear them, they could hear *him*. They would hear any sound he made.

"Nobody's around to see us," he heard a second voice growl. "Stop moaning."

That second voice sounded familiar, Tal thought. Even over the netcom ...

"What about that big fish-thing we saw with all the teeth?" asked a third voice. "Sometime that might be waitin' for us when we come up."

"If it is," said the growling second voice, "I'll blast it out of the water."

Tal's eyes went wider. The leading swimmer was holding up one of the ship's magno-rifles, which were supposed to be kept locked away.

"Just as I'd do," the growling voice went on, "to anything – or any*body* – that gets in our way."

Tal shivered as he cowered among the weeds while the three kept coming. But they swam on straight past the patch of weeds, without even looking at it.

Tal only just stopped himself from heaving a sigh of relief, which they certainly would have heard. The three swimmers were picking up speed and were soon out of sight, heading towards the Clear Zone and the starship.

Tal knew he should go back, too. But he wanted to let the others get well ahead of him, before he set off. Meanwhile, he could have a look around.

He slid out of the patch of weeds and swam towards the spot where he had seen the three strangers come up, as if out of the ground. There, beyond a sandy ridge, he saw an opening, like a gash in the ocean floor.

It was the mouth of a pit, about ten metres long, fairly narrow and far too dark to tell how deep it was. It had to be where the trio had come out.

But, Tal wondered, *why*? What could be down there?

He glanced around, to make sure he was alone, then moved closer to the pit's dark opening. There he flicked on his helmet light – and blinked with surprise.

Below him, the rough walls of the pit were dotted with tiny, gleaming points of light, like stars in the night sky.

Maybe it's metal ore, he thought, or shiny stones. Maybe it's something valuable.

He nerved himself to dive down into the pit's darkness, for a closer look. But first, he glanced around again. And sudden horror turned his blood to ice.

Some distance away, beside a small, sandy ridge, he saw a monstrous creature. And it was moving menacingly in his direction – as if it was hunting.

Chapter 5

Terror Attack

The monster was about the size of a large shark, but uglier. It had a massive body, many broad fins and a long, powerful tail, all covered in rough, bumpy skin.

Worse, its huge, blunt head seemed to be mostly mouth – a cavern of a mouth, filled with fangs the size of swords. And on its snout and over its head a line of long, sharp spikes grew, like a deadly crest.

But its small eyes, half-hidden in the thick skin, seemed quite weak. It didn't seem to notice Tal, who crouched frozen with fright beside the pit.

Tal didn't think that even his subsuit's metal skin could resist those giant fangs, or the terrible spikes. And he didn't want to risk finding out. Carefully, shakily, he drew back, hoping to slip away.

But the monster saw or sensed the movement. It opened its mouth to show all its fearsome rows of fangs and surged forward in a deadly charge.

Tal gasped and fled, at his subsuit's top

speed. But the monster came after him.
And it was faster.

When he reached the heap of rocks near
the energy field on the edge of the Zone,
Tal risked a backward glance – and almost
screamed. The horror was only a few
metres behind him, and gaining.

Frantically, Tal tried to move faster.
His whole body was flinching, as he waited
for those monstrous fangs to close on him.

But nothing happened. And when he
looked back again, astonishment struck
him like a blow. The monster had stopped
chasing him. It had turned away and was
drifting among the heap of rocks.

What seemed like a cloud of fine sand

had somehow been stirred up around it, so Tal couldn't see *why* it had stopped. But just then he didn't care. He hurtled on and soon flashed through the energy field, back into the safety of the Clear Zone.

And also he felt weak with relief and leftover shock, he didn't slow down until he got back to the starship.

The giant, oval shape of the starship floated half-submerged like a metal island, with its upper levels rising high into the planet's misty air. Tal went wearily through the double hatch of the underwater airlock. Then he paused and slowly got out of his subsuit, which became heavy and clumsy with its power shut off.

He was worried about being spotted by the three unknown swimmers who had been out beyond the Zone. But the narrow corridors were silent and empty as he went along, lugging the suit. Everyone was busily at work, as usual.

And when Tal reached the cramped quarters that he shared with his Dad, he went to work himself.

He went to his computer, which was linked to the ship's computer network. In a moment he had called up a map of the Clear Zone, to see where he had been. The map showed that he had been in Sector 81c, which lay on the edge of the Zone and extended some way beyond it. So he called up the data on that sector.

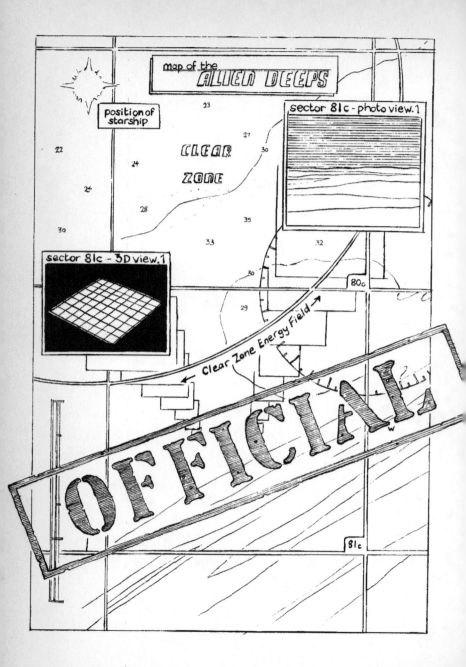

Chapter 6
Sector 81c

The computer network held detailed
records of all the exploration being done in
that alien ocean. Every single thing that
had been discovered, by the ship's scientists
or the robot drones, was noted in that data.

Yet the data, including photos, showed
that there was nothing at all in Sector 81c
except flat and empty sand.

No heap of rocks with octo-clowns. No tangled patch of weeds. No huge fanged monsters. *Definitely* no mysterious pit.

Tal blinked, frowned and double-checked. But it was the right location. And the photos, taken by a robot drone, were perfectly clear.

Yet the photos were showing that there was nothing at all worth looking at, out where he'd had his scary adventure.

It must be some kind of mix-up, he thought. After all, those three men had actually been *in* the pit. And they had talked about the monster. So *they* would know the records were wrong ...

At that moment his Dad burst through

the door. "There you are!" his Dad said cheerfully. "Come on – we'll be late for dinner!" He swept Tal off to the upper-level area where everyone – scientists and crew, all two dozen of them – had their evening meal together.

After they collected their food from the robot servers, he and his Dad sat down at the long table where everyone sat. But although Tal was painfully hungry he didn't start eating at once. Because he had heard a rough, growling voice that he thought he recognised.

It sounded like the voice of the unknown swimmer who had been carrying the magno-rifle. And it belonged to a big, hard-faced man named Saltro, sitting near the other end of the table.

Chapter 7
Under Suspicion

Saltro was chief officer of the crew. So he was second-in-command to the captain, the leader of the whole expedition, a tall woman who sat at the top of the table.

Tal had never had much to do with Saltro, nor with the two crewmen who were his special friends – a bony man named Vellit and a stocky man named Bann.

But as he listened, Tal was sure he recognised all three of their voices, from those scary moments beyond the Zone.

Then his Dad nudged him. "What have you been doing today?" he asked.

"Not much," Tal said carefully. "I went swimming. Then ... I looked through some exploration records. And I saw something really strange in the data on Sector 81c, out on the edge of the Zone."

Those words made several people nearby turn towards him with mild interest. Saltro and his two friends went suddenly quiet, began staring at Tal and started scowling.

A young woman sitting opposite laughed. "It's an alien world, Tal," she teased. "It's *all* strange."

"I know that," Tal said, annoyed. "But in the photos 81c looks like nothing, just flat and empty. No rocks, no tall weeds ..."

He stopped himself, but it was too late. His annoyance had made him say more than he should have. And Saltro and his friends were wearing even darker scowls.

"Why d'you think there should be rocks and weeds there, boy?" Saltro snapped. "You been swimming there, on the Zone's edge?"

Tal gulped. "It ... it just looked emptier than other places. On the *computer* ..."

"I do hope you haven't forgotten, Tal," the tall captain said, "that you mustn't ever swim out of sight of the ship."

"No," Tal muttered, wishing he hadn't spoken.

Saltro's friend Vellit snorted. "Come off it. Kids are always goin' where they're not supposed to. I'd bet good money he's been out to the edge!"

Tal's Dad gave him a worried look. "You haven't, have you, son?"

Tal stared down at his plate, unable to lie to his Dad. "Only for a minute or so ..." he mumbled.

Saltro glared. "An alien ocean's no place for a kid who won't obey orders," he snarled. "We ought to take away his subsuit, keep him out of trouble."

The captain nodded. "You may be right," she said. "Young people are curious and easily tempted."

But as Tal looked horrified she smiled and went on. "Still we can't keep an active boy inside the starship all the time. So I think, Tal, your father should take charge of your subsuit. You may still go swimming, but only near the ship – and from now on, always with an adult. You must *never again* swim alone."

Chapter 8

Escape into Danger

After that, nearly everyone went back to talking about other things. Tal was glad that he didn't have to face any more questions. But Saltro and his friends were still scowling at him. And his Dad was looking upset.

After dinner, his Dad gave him a firm talking-to about obeying orders. Then he put Tal's subsuit away in a locker and sent him to bed.

Tal wished he'd never gone near Sector 81c. At least, he thought gloomily, no one knows I went *out* of the Clear Zone. It didn't occur to anyone that I'd dare to break *that* rule.

But it wasn't against the rules for a group of adults to swim wherever they wished. So why hadn't Saltro and his mates said that *they* had been in Sector 81c? It must be, he said to himself, because they're up to something that they want to keep secret ...

Tal sat up sharply as another idea came to him. What if Saltro had somehow changed the computer records? He could have put in false pictures of Sector 81c, to make it look flat and empty and boring. To *hide* something. Like ... a mysterious pit.

So, he asked himself again, what could be down there, in the pit?

Over the next few days the question kept nagging at him. And it didn't help that he had to spend much of that time on his jobs around the starship or doing schoolwork with the Compu-Tutor.

In fact, during those days, Tal went swimming only twice, both times with his Dad, just around the ship.

That had been fairly boring – but not swimming at all was even worse, when he was *aching* to go and explore the mystery of the pit.

But his boredom ended unexpectedly one morning. Tal's Dad was looking for a jar full of tiny, twisted shells gathered from the ocean. After much rooting around, he found it in the locker where Tal's subsuit was kept. Snatching up the jar, he hurried off to his work. And he forgot to lock the door of the locker.

Tal stared at the door for a breathless moment. Then he flung it open, snatched the subsuit and ran. He half-expected to be stopped, but as usual the ship's corridors were silent and empty.

In the lower airlock he kicked off his shoes and pulled on the heavy suit over his

T-shirt and shorts. Then he switched on the suit's power, opened the hatch and plunged into the dimness of the alien sea.

Tal knew how much trouble he'd be in if he was caught. But he'd be quick, he told himself. He'd just dash out and have a good look at that pit, then get back into the ship before anyone missed him.

He rushed away at full speed, flashing through the water like a long, sleek fish. In a short while he reached the edge of the Clear Zone and swept on through the energy field without a pause.

As Tal paused by the heap of rocks, he saw a few octo-clowns floating there, eye patches flashing. But he ignored them and rushed on to the edge of the pit. His heart was racing and his teeth were clenched as he swam over the pit's dark opening and dived.

As the blackness gathered around him, he decided to risk using his helmet light. He touched the switch – and blinked in surprise.

When he had looked into the pit the first time, he had seen an enormous number of points of gleaming light. But now, just a few days later, there was only a handful left, widely scattered on the pit's walls.

He tried to think what could have happened. But then in the next moment, his puzzlement turned to raw terror.

Below, in the depths of the pit, three subsuited figures lunged out from under a ledge and surged upwards with their hands reaching to grab him.

Chapter 9

Grip of the Enemy

In panic, Tal shot up out of the pit and streaked away. That flash of speed took him into the patch of tangled weeds before the three figures reached the top of the pit. Their helmet lights flared out through the water, but by that time Tal was well-hidden. Carefully, he slid out of the weeds on the far side, then shot away towards the heap of rocks, still unseen.

"I *knew* that kid must've been pokin' around here, before!" said the voice of Saltro's mate Vellit, which made Tal jump as it crackled out of his netcom.

"Little sneak – creepin' around, spyin' ..." That was the third one, Bann.

"Stop talking and *move*!" That was Saltro's angry growl. "We have to get him before he reaches the ship!"

In among the rocks, Tal ducked into the little cave where he had been surrounded by octo-clowns. There he huddled in the darkness and watched the three helmet lights draw closer.

"What's that over there?" he heard Vellit say.

"Just one of those clown things," Saltro snarled. "Come *on*!"

The three helmet lights swept over the rocks, but failed to reach into the cave where Tal huddled. Then they moved on and the water grew dim again.

"We should spot him inside the Zone ..." he heard Bann mutter.

Then the voice cut off. Most likely, Tal thought, because the three men had crossed into the Zone. So they had gone through the energy field that blocked all netcom contact.

For several moments Tal stayed where he was without moving. But at last he slid nervously forward to the mouth of the cave. He was desperate to get back to the safety of the ship. But what if Saltro and the others were waiting to ambush him on the way? Maybe if I go around, he thought, to come from the other direction ...

Slowly, Tal eased himself out of the cave. Then he cried out in new terror, as powerful hands clamped on to his arms.

"Got you!" a voice growled over the netcom. And as Tal was spun around, he saw that it was Saltro gripping him. Tal also flinched at the sight of the magno-rifle over Saltro's shoulder and the murderous scowl on his face.

The other two crowded around. "You were right, Saltro," Vellit said. "He was tryin' to hide, instead of runnin'."

"Let go of me!" Tal said fearfully.

"Oh, I will," Saltro growled. "Very soon."

"You goin' to let him *go*?" Bann asked, puzzled.

Saltro's grin was cruel. "In a way. I'm going to let him discover what he wants to know. He'll be able to see exactly what's down there, in the pit."

"But he'll *tell*!" Bann said, even more puzzled.

"No," Saltro snarled. "Because he won't get *out* of the pit. Not ever."

Chapter 10
Into Darkness

In a frenzy, Tal began to struggle against the fierce grip that held him. As he kicked and thrashed, he almost broke free. But then the other two grabbed him as well and held him tightly.

And Saltro, his grin still glinting through his face-plate, reached over and switched off the power of Tal's subsuit.

Without power, the suit at once became a stiff, heavy mass. Tal could hardly move because of the weight of the suit as the three men swam away from the heap of rocks, pulling him along.

He was still able to breathe, thanks to the emergency tank of stored air. But he knew that small store wouldn't last long. Also, his netcom was still working. It had its own tiny power source that kept it switched on all the time. So, in panic, he begged them to let him go. But they just laughed nastily and swam on.

"Are you goin' to shoot him?" Bann asked. "Or pull his helmet off and drown him?"

"That'd be too quick," Saltro said, "after all the trouble he's caused us."

He reached a hand down to the main power switch on Tal's subsuit, twisting and crushing it. Under that pressure, the switch crumpled and snapped – to become a useless patch of metal that could never turn on the suit again.

"This way," Saltro growled,"if he's found later it'll look like an accident."

"They'd better not find him too quick," Vellit grumbled. "He's still got his netcom."

"By the time they get worried enough to start a search," Saltro snapped, "the kid's air will have run out. And they might never find him at all, at the bottom of the pit."

Total horror swept over Tal, so that he couldn't move or make a sound. He simply lay still within the dead suit, numb and wild-eyed, as they swam on.

In a few moments they reached the pit and floated above its inky depths.

"There's still some crystals left," Vellit said.

"We'll take them now," Saltro said. He laughed harshly. "Anyway, we've already got enough xantium to make three *thousand* people rich."

Despite his terror, Tal twitched with shock. Xantium! The alien crystals that were vital to all spaceflight among the stars ... the most priceless treasure in the galaxy! *That's* what those points of light were in the walls of the pit!

Saltro and his pals must have discovered them, he thought, but hadn't told anyone. They were taking the crystals for themselves, making themselves rich ... But that thought faded, as Saltro pushed his face-plate up to Tal's.

"You should've kept out of our business, boy," he snarled. "You should've stayed near the starship, like you were told."

Still, silenced by horror, Tal could only stare blankly as Saltro drew back. Then all three men took their hands away and let him go.

They switched on their helmet lights and watched, grinning, as Tal began to sink within the dead weight of his suit.

Down, down he sank into the darkness of the pit.

At last, Tal did scream, in total mind-shattering terror. But still he sank, within the suit's deadly weight – bathed in the glare of the three helmet lights above him.

He screamed again, though he knew it was useless. No one could hear him except his three enemies. He would sink to the bottom of the pit and lie there in the ooze, unable to move as he waited for the last of his air to run out.

He might *never* be found, ever. His Dad might never know what happened to him. And the three evil men above would get away with their crime and with the xantium ...

Just then the three helmet lights at the top of the pit pulled away suddenly. The men may have got tired of watching, or had gone to collect the last xantium crystals from the pit walls. And as Tal stared in terror up at the patch of grey dimness that was the top of the pit, he shrieked once more, with even greater fear.

Something moved across that greyness. The enormous, shadowy shape of the fanged, spiky monster that had chased him before.

Chapter 11
Out of Darkness

The monster had to be the reason why the watching men had left. But Tal was no longer thinking about the men in his new horror, as the monster swept down into the pit.

Nor did he notice a faint weird *glow* around the monster – as if there were lights behind it. But not helmet lights. They were softer and smaller, glowing and winking ...

As the monster speared down at him, all Tal could do was take a breath to scream one final time ...

But he made no sound. Because, to his complete surprise, the monster didn't attack him.

Instead, it swirled past him. And then at last Tal clearly saw the lights that were glowing behind its bulk. Octo-clowns – about eight of them, with their eye patches flashing like neon.

Their spindly tentacles were gripping some of the bumps on the monster's rough skin, so that they were riding it. And, somehow, *guiding* it.

Tal remembered seeing octo-clowns by the rocks when Saltro grabbed him. And, he thought, they've come to help. It might even have been octo-clowns who stopped the monster chasing me before.

He gasped. The monster had halted beneath him and was slowly floating upwards, until it lifted Tal on to its broad back.

Then it kept rising, carrying him up carefully through the pit's dark water, guided by its octo-clown riders.

Tal still lay unmoving inside the dead suit as the monster brought him up out of the pit. And then it swam away with him – towards the energy field on the edge of the Clear Zone.

Tal couldn't make out how the octo-clowns were controlling it. Perhaps with *mind* power, he thought. But that would mean something quite remarkable, something that no one on the starship had ever guessed at.

The clowns must be *intelligent* aliens. Maybe the flashing eye patches were their way of speaking. So, one day, humans might be able to speak *with* them ...

In that instant, as if to offer proof, the clowns made the giant monster do something startling, and perfectly timed. As it swam near to the energy field, they urged it to go faster. Then, at the last second, they swerved it sharply away from the field.

The swerve flung Tal off the monster's back, so that he went flying through the energy field and into the Clear Zone.

Clearly the octo-clowns couldn't take the monster through the energy field, which would have shocked them all. Instead, they had managed to throw Tal through. As if they knew that he would be safe there.

As his forward motion slowed to a gentle drift, Tal peered nervously around, but saw no sign of his three enemies. He saw no sign of them. Instead, to his delight, he heard voices, calling.

Now that he was back in the Zone, he was in netcom contact again. And the voices were search parties out looking for him. He could hear one desperate voice in particular – raw and hoarse, as it called his name. His Dad.

"Dad!" Tal yelled as loudly as he could. "I'm here! I'm *here*!"

All the shouts turned at once to cries of relief and joy, his Dad's loudest of all. In the distance he saw helmet lights flaring, as the searchers rushed towards him.

He realised then that his air was running out – but he'd be back in the starship before it was all gone. He also saw that the octo-clowns and the huge monster had flashed away through the dim waters, out of sight.

But we'll meet again, he thought happily. And *I'll* find a way to say thank you …

Tal sighed as he lay back in the useless suit. Dad and everyone will be really furious with me, he thought, for disobeying orders and sneaking off. But not for long. Not after I tell them about Saltro and the others. And about the xantium crystals that will make us *all* rich. And about finding out that the octo-clowns are intelligent …

I won't be punished then, he smiled to himself. I'll be a *hero*.

Barrington Stoke would like to thank all its readers for commenting on the manuscript before publication and in particular:

David Andrews
Pete Bearcroft
Harry Brough
Susan Carston
Jai Cruickshanks
Lynette Ferguson
A. Galloway
Scott Marks
Carolina Maxwell
Philip Veneruso

Become a Consultant!

Would you like to give us feedback on our titles before they are published? Contact us at the address or website below – we'd love to hear from you!

Barrington Stoke, 10 Belford Terrace, Edinburgh EH4 3DQ
Tel: 0131 315 4933 Fax: 0131 315 4934
E-mail: barringtonstoke@cs.com
Website: www.barringtonstoke.co.uk

More Titles

Playing Against the Odds
by Bernard Ashley

Chris's world is turned upside down by the arrival of Fiona in his class. His loyalties are torn in two as more and more thefts take place at school. But nothing can prepare Chris for the betrayal that lies ahead ...

The Shadow on The Stairs
by Ann Halam

People say Joe's new house is haunted. Every night, he looks for the shadow on the attic stairs. Sometimes he thinks he can see it, sometimes he knows he can't. He tells himself that he isn't scared and wishes he could get the idea that it is evil out of his mind ...

Runaway Teacher
by Pete Johnson

Scott thinks teachers are boring. Then a new teacher arrives - a teacher with very different ideas about lessons, rules and school. But when too many rules are broken, Scott learns just how complicated friendship and loyalty can be.

Falling Awake
by Viv French

Danny is cool. The younger kids think they're cool too, but they are just kiddie babes to Danny. He can make easy money out of them. He isn't going to say no to easy money, is he? Not until the day he wakes up on the pavement. Out of it. Trapped. This time Danny's gone too far.

To Be A Millionaire
by Yvonne Coppard

The news that a famous film director is in town sets Jack's mind racing. At last, he thinks, he's finally got his break! All he has to do is to be in the right place at the right time. This time it's up to him.